Mercer Mayer's
A Monster Followed Me to School

To Frank and Kathy Skiles,
another monster just for you

Mercer Mayer's
A Monster Followed Me to School

A GOLDEN BOOK • NEW YORK
Western Publishing Company, Inc., Racine, Wisconsin 53404

There was a monster on our block. One day he was just there. I know because I saw him on my way home from school. I was scared that first time, so I ran away.

Before dinner I told my dad. But a monster on our block didn't seem to bother my dad at all. He just smiled and patted me on the head.

Later on, he said I should spend more time figuring out how to do well at school and less time on monsters.

I asked if I could be excused from the table.

After dinner I told my mom. She said it was probably the same monster that used to live under my bed.

I told her this monster looked a lot different.
My mom asked me to explain, but I went to my
room to put on my pajamas instead.

The next day I started walking to school like always. But pretty soon I had a funny feeling that my monster might be following me. He was.

He looked hungry. I didn't want to hang around with him if he was hungry. I figured he might do something weird all of a sudden. So I got out my lunch and gave it to him.

He ate the whole thing, bag and all. Then he burped.

Then he looked right at me and smiled. I
mean he really smiled. That's when I decided he
liked me.

I had to get going, so I started walking again. My monster walked right behind me, but nobody seemed to notice. Not one person said anything, not even the postman.

When I got to school, Biff was waiting for me.
He's the school bully. Biff has been pushing me
around ever since I was a little kid.

Biff walked up to me. All of a sudden my monster happened to swing his tail around. Biff's legs flew right out from under him. He fell down, and everyone laughed.

Biff thought I did it. He was pretty mad. He told me I was going to get it after school.

I opened my knapsack and got out the book I'd borrowed from Amy Frobish. But my monster grabbed the book right out of my hand and tried to eat it.

When I gave Amy her book, she said she was going to show it to the teacher.

I'm always getting in trouble.

At school, my monster climbed right on top of the teacher's desk. Then he lay there making faces and sticking out his tongue.

Boy, oh, boy, I thought. Would he ever get in trouble if the teacher saw him doing that. She would tell him he'd better be careful. His face could freeze that way.

Thinking of that made me laugh, which meant I got in trouble. I had to write I WILL BE QUIET IN CLASS twenty-five times on the blackboard.

My monster got tired of waiting for me, so he blew all the papers off the teacher's desk.

She rushed over to close the window. But the window wasn't open.

At recess my monster spent a lot of time on the slide. He even took turns.

I thought that was great.

Then he played kickball for a while. The best part was when he tripped Biff. Of course, Biff was sure I did it. Boy was he mad. "You're really going to get it!" he yelled.

We were supposed to watch a video called
Birds of Brazil, but the teacher couldn't find it.
My monster was getting hungry again. I think he
ate the video.

We didn't do our work sheets because the teacher couldn't find those, either. My monster probably ate those, too. We drew pictures instead. I drew a picture of my monster. Everyone thought it was dumb.

Then we practiced the song my teacher wrote for Parent's Night. This is how it started:

"When I give my everything,

I have a happy song to sing."

I'm not too crazy about the song.

My monster didn't want to be left out, so he sang along. He didn't really sing. He howled, and it sounded terrible. The teacher kept looking in our direction. I think she couldn't figure out what was going on.

I didn't sing very well, either. If my monster and I sang together a lot, all the kids in my class would probably move away.

After singing practice, my monster left the room. I think he was bored. Or hungry.

The next time I saw him was at lunch in the cafeteria. He waved at me. Then he reached into a big pot of chicken à la king and licked his paw. That was okay with me. I hate chicken à la king.

I bought myself a bag of potato chips. I had to get something because my monster had eaten my lunch.

I'm pretty sure our principal saw him later
that day. I was just standing there. The principal
went running down the hall, moaning.

They said he went home after that.

In the afternoon, Amy Frobish showed her
beat-up book to the teacher. The teacher made
me stay after the bell and write

I WILL TAKE GOOD CARE

OF THINGS I BORROW

twenty-five times on the blackboard.

Then I had to erase the whole blackboard
before the teacher would let me leave.

When I finally got out of school, Biff was waiting for me. He was going to beat me up. Everyone was there to watch what happened, even Amy Frobish. First I thought I would run back inside of the school building and hide, but I'd just have to come out sooner or later. Then I thought maybe I should just faint and lie on the ground real still. But then everyone would say I was chicken. No, I decided, I'd just have to get beat up. Then the strangest thing happened.

Biff looked in my direction, and his eyes got big. His mouth dropped open. Then he ran off down the street.

I turned around. There was my monster, right behind me. I guess Biff could see him, too.

What a great feeling. The two of us were too much for Biff.

I started home. I knew my monster was behind me. I figured he'd walk the whole way with me.

When the light turned green, I crossed the street like I always do. But my monster didn't cross behind me. He stayed on the other side, near school.

I watched for a while to see what he was going to do. What he did was turn around and walk back to the school building.

I figured he liked school. Or maybe it was the cafeteria.

BUS STOP

When I got home, I told my mom what happened. She said school was a good place for a monster. She liked the part about the principal running down the hall.

When my dad got home, I didn't tell him what happened. I didn't think he'd like the part about me writing things twenty-five times.

One thing was sure. I was never going to borrow anything from Amy Frobish ever again.

Before it got completely dark, I went outside. I rode my bike around the block just to double-check. My monster wasn't anywhere. We definitely don't have a monster on our block anymore.

He's at my school. I think he lives in the basement there, because this winter the boiler has broken down three times so far. Our janitor always makes his assistant go down there, and our principal quit. They told us he had a medical problem, but I don't think so.

Biff doesn't hit me anymore. He even crosses the street when he sees me coming, which is great. I hope he keeps it up.

I'm even friends with Amy Frobish again.

I'm glad the monster followed me to school. I
miss him sometimes. I might want to try to find
him again, someday. If I do...

...I can always go down to the school basement and check behind the boiler.

A Note to Parents

Dorling Kindersley Readers is a compelling new program for beginning readers, designed in conjunction with leading literacy experts, including Dr. Linda Gambrell, President of the National Reading Conference and past board member of the International Reading Association.

Beautiful illustrations and superb full-color photographs combine with engaging, easy-to-read stories to offer a fresh approach to each subject in the series. Each *Dorling Kindersley Reader* is guaranteed to capture a child's interest while developing his or her reading skills, general knowledge, and love of reading.

The four levels of *Dorling Kindersley Readers* are aimed at different reading abilities, enabling you to choose the books that are exactly right for your child:

Level 1 – Beginning to read
Level 2 – Beginning to read alone
Level 3 – Reading alone
Level 4 – Proficient readers

The "normal" age at which a child begins to read can be anywhere from three to eight years old, so these levels are intended only as a general guideline.

No matter which level you select, you can be sure that you are helping your child learn to read, then read to learn!

DK

LONDON, NEW YORK, SYDNEY, DELHI, PARIS,
MUNICH, and JOHANNESBURG

Produced by Southern Lights
Custom Publishing

For DK
Publisher Andrew Berkhut
Executive Editor Mary Atkinson
Art Director Tina Vaughan
Photographer Keith Harrelson

Reading Consultant
Linda Gambrell, Ph.D.

First American Edition, 2001
03 04 05 06 10 9 8 7 6 5 4 3 2
Published in the United States by
DK Publishing, Inc.
95 Madison Avenue, New York, New York 10016

Library of Congress Cataloging-in-Publication Data
Hayward, Linda.
   A day in the life of a reporter / written by Linda Hayward. --
1st American ed.
   p. cm.
   ISBN 0-7894-7956-7 -- ISBN 0-7894-7957-5 (pbk.)
   1. Television broadcasting of news--Juvenile literature.
   2. Reporters and reporting—Juvenile literature I. Title.

PN4784.T4 H39 2001
070.1'95--dc21   2001017392

Printed and bound in China by L. Rex Printing Co., Ltd.

The publisher would like to thank the following for their kind permission to reproduce their
photographs:
Key: t=top, b=bottom, l=left, r=right, c=center
DK Picture Library: Dave King front cover. Models: Stephanie Aaron, Mae Bethea, Anna
Cowan, Kapil Desai, Steve Gates, Gonzalo Garmendi, Natalia Garmendi, Andrea Hand,
Christopher Holby, Tim Jones, Duke LaGrone, Thomas Lower, Ben Philpott, Cassandra Porter,
Mira Rubin, Haley Spratt, and Marliese Thomas.

In addition, Dorling Kindersley would like to thank Shirley Harden and ABC 33/40,
Birmingham, Alabama for location photography, and Joe Miele of Diamond Studios for props.

see our complete
catalog at
www.dk.com

DORLING KINDERSLEY *READERS*

BEGINNING **1** TO READ

A Day in the Life of a TV Reporter

Written by Linda Hayward

DK Publishing, Inc.

Mark Garcia listens to the radio
as he gets ready for work.
He needs to know the news.
Mark is a TV reporter.

Mark's daughter, Sara, gets ready for school.

Mark takes Sara to school.
Then he goes to the TV station.

At the TV station, Mark sees Jen.
She works the camera.

camera

"Are you ready
for the news-team meeting?"
asks Jen.
"Yes," says Mark.

The team decides what stories to report for tonight's news. Mark says that a local school is cleaning up a river.

Laurie is the producer.
She is in charge of the news.
"Mark and Jen can report
on the clean up," says Laurie.

videotape

Mark finds
an old videotape.
It shows how clean
the river used to be.

He writes some notes
about the videotape
in his notebook.
He can use them
in his report.

notebook

Mark and Jen drive to the river.
Lots of people are there.
Mark starts talking
to the students.
Jen starts videotaping.

Mark's cell phone rings.
"How's the clean up going?"
asks Laurie, the producer.
"It's going well," says Mark.
"It will be a good story."

cell
phone

Mark sees Ellen and Steve
from the local newspaper.
They are interviewing
one of the students.

Ben is a reporter
from a radio station.
He is recording the story
on a tape recorder.

tape
recorder

Jen points the camera at Mark.
"People used to swim in this river,
but now it is full of trash,"
says Mark.

Jen points the camera
at the students.
"Today these students
are cleaning up the river,"
Mark says.

Page and Libby
are picking up cans.
Page sometimes baby-sits Sara,
Mark's daughter.
She sees Mark and waves to him.

Mark holds
the microphone
up to Page.

microphone

"What do you want to see?"
he asks.
"A clean river!" cries Page.

Suddenly there is a shout.
"Look what I found!" calls Libby.
She holds up a metal box.
It has jewelry and money inside!

Jen takes a shot of Libby
with the box.
"We'll put this on the news,"
says Mark.
"Maybe we'll find the owner!"

Mark and Jen are excited.
"This is a big story now,"
says Jen.

They pack up the camera
and go back to the TV station.

Brian, the technician, edits
the tape on the TV screen.
Mark tells Brian
which parts to use.

TV screen

Now the story is ready
for the news.
Mark leaves to pick up Sara
from school.

At home, Sara and Mark
talk about the day.
"Did you see Page?" asks Sara.
"Yes," says Mark.
"Her friend found
a box of treasure!"

Back at the TV station,
the cameras and studio lights
are on.

lights

Max, the director, makes sure
everything happens on time.
He tells Bob to start reading
the news.

"There was an exciting find at the river clean up today," says Bob.

After the news,
Mark's phone rings.
It is Laurie, the producer.

"The box of jewelry and money
was stolen property," says Laurie.
"The lady who owns it
called the station.
She's giving the money
to the river clean up!"

"Dad, you did a great job!"
says Sara.
"I can't wait to tell
everyone at school!"

Mark smiles.
He has the best job in the world.

Picture Word List

camera page 7

tape recorder page 15

videotape page 10

microphone page 19

notebook page 11

TV screen page 24

cell phone page 13

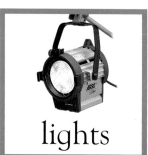

lights page 27